WHICH
ONE
IS
WHITNEY?

Which One Is Whitney?

by James Stevenson

 Greenwillow Books, New York

for LIZ

Watercolor paints and a black pen were used for
the full-color art.
The text type is ITC Modern.

Printed in Hong Kong by South China
Printing Company (1988) Ltd.

First Edition   1 2 3 4 5 6 7 8 9 10

Library of Congress Cataloging-in-Publication Data
Stevenson, James (date)
Which one is Whitney? / James Stevenson.
p.   cm.
Summary: Follows the amusing adventures of Whitney, a
clever dugong, as he tries to find his place in the world.
ISBN 0-688-09061-3
ISBN 0-688-09062-1 (lib. bdg.)
[1. Dugong—Fiction.]   I. Title.
PZ7.S84748Whi   1990
[E]—dc20   89-34614   CIP   AC

1

WHICH ONE IS WHITNEY?

"What a lovely family you have,
Mrs. Dugong," said Mrs. Grouper.
"Now remind me—which one is
which?"

"Well," said Mrs. Dugong, "Warren's the cheerful one. Winnie's the polite one. Wally's the friendly one. Wendy's the funny one. And then there's Whitney…"

"Which one is Whitney?" asked Mrs. Grouper.

"Whitney," whispered Mrs. Dugong,
"is the one who isn't <u>quite</u> so cheerful,
or polite, or friendly, or funny."
"I see," said Mrs. Grouper.

Whitney heard what his mother said.
He paddled off alone.

Mrs. Grouper swam home. "Warren's
the cheerful one," she said to herself.
"Winnie's the polite one. Wally's the
friendly one. Wendy's the funny one.
And Whitney—he's none of the above."

Then she saw one of the Dugong children.

"Hi, Mrs. Grouper," said the Dugong. "How are you? Nice to see you! <u>Always</u> nice to see you!"

"Hello," said Mrs. Grouper. "You must be...Wally?"

"Right!" said Wally, and he swam away.

Another Dugong came by. "Want to
hear a good joke, Mrs. Grouper?" asked
the Dugong.
"Maybe later…Wendy," said
Mrs. Grouper.
"Okay," said Wendy, and she swam away.

"Hello," said Mrs. Grouper, as another
Dugong came by.
"Greetings, Mrs. Grouper," said the
Dugong. "Doesn't the water feel
wonderful today?"
"Yes, it does, Warren," said Mrs. Grouper.

A few minutes later, Mrs. Grouper
nearly bumped into another Dugong.
"Oh, excuse me, Mrs. Grouper!" said the
Dugong. "I'm terribly sorry—my fault!"
"That's perfectly all right, Winnie," said
Mrs. Grouper.

Later that morning, Mrs. Grouper saw
Mrs. Dugong again.
"I've run into all your children, except
for Whitney," said Mrs. Grouper, "and
I think I know which is which."
"But they've all been with <u>me</u> all
morning," said Mrs. Dugong,
"except for Whitney."

"But I talked to each <u>one</u>!" said Mrs. Grouper. "Except for Whitney."

"Well, ask them yourself," said Mrs. Dugong. "Winnie, come here!"

"Yes, Mother," said Winnie.

"Didn't I run into you this morning, Winnie?" asked Mrs. Grouper.

"No, Mrs. Grouper," said Winnie. "I'm sure I would remember such a nice surprise."

"Wendy!" called Mrs. Dugong.

"Hi, Mrs. Grouper," said Wendy.

"Didn't you try to tell me a joke this
morning?" asked Mrs. Grouper.

"No, Mrs. Grouper," said Wendy, "but I
could tell you one now."

"Not now, Wendy," said Mrs. Dugong.

"Warren!" called Mrs. Dugong.

Warren swam over.

"Warren," said Mrs. Grouper, "didn't we meet somewhere this morning?"

"No, Mrs. Grouper," said Warren, "but it would have been a great pleasure to see you!"

"Hi there, Mrs. Grouper!" said Wally.

"Delighted to see you!"

"Here's Wally," said Mrs. Dugong.

"Did I bump into you this morning, Wally?" asked Mrs. Grouper.

"I wish you had, Mrs. Grouper," said Wally, "but no."

"That's everybody, except Whitney," said
　Mrs. Dugong.

"It's all very strange," said Mrs.
　Grouper. "Very strange indeed."

"Here comes Whitney now," said Mrs.
　Dugong.

"Whitney," said Mrs. Grouper, "did we
　meet this morning?"

"Several times, Mrs. Grouper," said
　Whitney. "But it's always nice to see
　you again!" He waved and swam off.

"And how do you tell which one is
Whitney, again?" asked Mrs. Grouper,
as they watched him swim away.
"At the moment," said Mrs. Dugong,
"I'm beginning to think that Whitney
may be a little bit more...clever than
the rest."
"I think you're right," said Mrs. Grouper.

2
HELP WITH THE KELP

"Today, children," said Mrs. Dugong,
"you're all going to help with the kelp."
"Again, Mother?" said Wally. "We helped
with the kelp last month."
"If we don't keep clearing out the kelp,"
said Mrs. Dugong, "we'll get all tangled
up in it."

"I'll curl kelp," said Winnie.

"I'll carry kelp," said Wally.

"I'll help curl kelp," said Wendy.

"I'll help carry kelp," said Warren.

"That's nice," said Mrs. Dugong.

"Let's get started!"

"What about Whitney?" said Winnie.

"Doesn't Whitney have to help with
the kelp?"

"Of course," said Mrs. Dugong.

"Where <u>is</u> Whitney?"

22

"When I saw him," said Wally,
"Whitney was bothering
  the barnacles."

"When I saw him," said Warren,
"he was messing with
  the mussels."

"I'll go find him," said Mrs. Dugong.
"You children keep cleaning up the
  kelp." She swam away.

Meanwhile,
Whitney was
jiggling
jellyfish.

Then he sneaked up
on some starfish.

Then he bumped into something large
and dark.

It was a large, dark stingray.

Whitney swam away as fast as he could—
into a forest of kelp, and kept going.

"Is that Whitney?" asked Winnie.

"I think so," said Warren.

"I never saw him work so hard,"
 said Winnie.

A moment later, Mrs. Dugong came
back. "My goodness," she said, "where's
all the kelp?"

"All gone," said Wally.

"Did Whitney help with the kelp?"
asked Mrs. Dugong.

"Yes," said Warren. "In fact, he did
it all alone."

"What a good boy you are," said
 Mrs. Dugong.
"I try," said Whitney.

3

THE MACKEREL MARATHON

"Hey, which one are you?" asked Mort the mackerel.

"I'm Whitney," said Whitney.

"Tomorrow's the annual Mackerel Marathon," said Mort. "Want to enter?"

"What is it?" asked Whitney.

"A race," said Mort. "Ten miles to Pirate's Rock."

"Probably not this year," said Whitney.
"What's the matter?" said Mort. "Too fat
and too slow?"
Mort and the other mackerels laughed.
"You Dugongs are all alike," said Mort,
and they all laughed again.

"On second thought," said Whitney,
"I think I <u>will</u> race."
"Okay, Whitney!" said Mort. "See
   you right here at the starting line
   tomorrow at seven."

The next morning everybody lined up.

"Ready! Get set! Go!" said Mort.

"So long, Whitney!" cried the mackerels.

"Let's break the record today!"
Mort said. "Everybody swim faster!"

"I can see Pirate's Rock!" yelled Mort.
"We're going to win!"

"Whitney!" said Mort. "How did you get here so fast?"

"A final burst of speed," said Whitney.

"I guess we should have swum faster,"
said Mort. "How did _we_ know he was
so fast?"
The mackerels swam away.

Whitney went home slowly.

"Did we win?" asked Warren, when
  Whitney arrived home.
"By miles," said Whitney. "You must
  have been great at the starting line."

"Thanks," said Warren, "but you were
  the one who had to swim all night
  to Pirate's Rock."
"I had lots of time," said Whitney. "It
  was a pleasant trip."
"Shhh," said Warren. "Here comes
  Mort."

"Tomorrow's <u>our</u> big race," said
 Whitney.
"What's that?" asked Mort.
"The Dugong Drifting Derby,"
 said Whitney. "Want to enter?"
"No more races," said Mort.

"I better start practicing," said Whitney,
and he closed his eyes. He drifted to
the left. Then he drifted to the right.
He drifted up, and he drifted down....